D1725474

The Pond

By Billy W. Cross
Illustrations by Blueberry Illustrations

Choose to live a happy life.
Keep your heart and mind open.
Say YES more than you say NO.
Dream big and then pursue.

Copyright © 2020 by Billy W. Cross

All rights reserved.
No part of this book may be reproduced
or transmitted in any form or by any means
without written permission from the author.

ISBN: 978-0-578-69739-0

This book is dedicated to my
mother, Marjorie E. Cross, who supported
my dreams throughout my childhood and to my
best friend, Dennet M. Withington, who has
supported my dreams all through my adult life.

When I was just a little boy,
Not even six years old,
My grandpa promised to take me to play
At a local swimming hole.

We started our journey down the railroad tracks,
Where the dirt was as red as brick.
Buzzing could be heard from the lumber mill,
And the air felt hot and thick.

We walked across a trestle,
That was high above a stream.
And we followed the tracks into the woods,
Where the trees shimmered emerald green.

Just as I started to get tired,
We had walked almost a mile.
Through the trees came the sound
of children laughing,
And I began to smile.

"We are almost there," my grandpa said,
As the sound of kids playing grew.
And when I peered through a thicket of trees,
I saw a sliver of blue.

My excitement grew as we left the tracks
And walked down a short rocky trail,
To the edge of the pond
where the children's laughter
Rang off the pond like a bell.

And in the radiant sunlight,
In a pond of brilliant blue,
Stood five naked ebony boys,
With smiles of the whitest hue.

The water looked like diamonds,
As it glistened on their skin.
And I knew I would have the time of my life,
As I shucked off my clothes to get in.

What happened next made my heart sink.
I wouldn't understand it till years later.
My grandpa told the Negro boys,
They would have to get out of the water.

Their smiles disappeared
and faces sank in defeat,
For they knew they had to obey.
They got out of the pond, put on their clothes,
And with heads down walked away.

Now all alone in the big blue pond,
I was far from having fun.
So after a while I turned to my grandpa and said,
"Okay, I'm done."

On the long walk home my grandpa explained,
Negroes are not equal to whites.
But even at that tender age,
I knew this couldn't be right.

Those boys were joyous and having fun,
Before my grandpa sent them home.
And if I was better than those boys,
Then why was I the one swimming alone?

Now my grandpa was my hero,
And in his eyes I saw no doubt.
So I took that lie into my heart,
And then spent years excising it out.

Historical Context

It is very important that your child understands the historical context of this story. The Pond depicts a real event that occurred in Birmingham, Alabama, in 1958. Still six years away from the Civil Rights Act of 1964, Alabama and many parts of the United States were still segregated. Blacks and whites could not attend the same schools, churches, theaters, or restaurants. They could not drink from the same water fountains or use the same restrooms. This separation was driven by America's slave history and racism.

Slave history: In 1619, a ship with twenty African captives landed in Jamestown, Virginia, ushering in the era of American slavery. Slavery officially ended in 1863 with the Civil War and the Emancipation Proclamation issued by Abraham Lincoln. While slavery officially ended, racism did not.

Racism: It refers to prejudice, discrimination, or antagonism directed against someone of a different race on the basis of the belief that one's own race is superior. In this context, whites believed they were superior or better than blacks. Some whites even, falsely, believed that blacks carried diseases that could be passed on to white people if they came in close contact with one another. As a result of racism and segregation (separation), African Americans have been severely disadvantaged in the United States.

Civil Rights Act of 1964: **This is the landmark civil rights and labor law in the United States that outlaws discrimination based on race, color, religion, sex, or national origin. It prohibits racial segregation in schools, employment, and public accommodations. First proposed by John F. Kennedy, the Civil Rights Act was signed into law by Lyndon B. Johnson.**

Martin Luther King Jr.: **He was an American Christian minister and activist who became the most visible spokesperson and leader for the Civil Rights Movement from 1955 until his assassination in 1968. He is mentioned here because we would not have the Civil Rights Act of 1964 without the Civil Rights Movement. Despite these advances, racism continues today and can be seen in many aspects of American life and culture.**

Glossary for The Pond

ebony – Very dark brown or blackish timber from a tropical tree (slang: dark skin tone).

excising – Removing something (usually by cutting it out). In this case it means to remove it or get it out.

glistening – Shining with a sparkling light.

lumber mill – A business where trees and raw wood are turned into planks, boards, plywood, and other wood products that are used in construction.

Negro – A member of a dark-skinned group or people originally native to Africa. A word used to refer to a black person before the term African American became acceptable.

shucked – Stripped off or removed, like stripping the husk from corn.

swimming hole – A place in a pond, stream, creek, river, or lake that is slow-moving and deep enough to swim.

thicket – A dense group of bushes or trees.

trestle – An open crossed-braced framework used to support an elevated structure such as a bridge for railroad tracks or roads.

Billy W. Cross was born on February 24, 1953, in Birmingham, Alabama. At the age of eleven he started performing for Birmingham Children's Theater where he developed a love for acting. He performed various roles for local theater companies throughout Alabama. At the age of nineteen, he moved to Hollywood in California to pursue a film career. Unable to make a living doing bit parts in movies, Billy moved to San Bernardino, California, to manage a local bookstore. After a few years, Billy went back to school to pursue a nursing career and was a licensed vocational nurse for twenty-seven years. In 2001, Billy retired from nursing, went back to college, and received a master's degree in education. He became a special education teacher for first through third grades. In 2018, after fifteen years, he retired from teaching. Still living in San Bernardino, California, Billy is now an author of children's books. He believes his love for rhyme and poetry comes from his mother, Marjorie E. Cross, who herself wrote rhyming poetry ever since she was a young girl. Billy was further inspired by the Canadian poet Robert W. Service who, through rhyme, could tell vivid and detailed stories.

CPSIA information can be obtained
at www.ICGtesting.com
Printed in the USA
BVHW021747160720
583884BV00015B/306